Being Mindful Like Grandpa

Sheri Mabry   illustrated by Ilaria Urbinati

Albert Whitman & Company
Chicago, Illinois

Each fall when the leaves
begin to change color,
Mom, Dad, and I hike up
the mountain with Grandpa.

This year everything is different. We're moving away from my school and my friends and from Grandpa. My worries feel like they're piled higher than the boxes in the back of the moving truck.

Before we leave, Grandpa gives me
a stone made smooth from the stream.

"Keep this in your pocket," he says. "When
you have worry-thoughts, rub the calming
stone between your fingers, and think of
something that makes you feel thankful."

Now, miles away from Grandpa, I slide the stone into my pocket.
Mom, Dad, and I start out on a path we've never hiked before.

Words Grandpa said follow me.

"Buddy. I know you are worried about all of the changes...
but you'll be okay."

But what if I'm not?

I crouch down by a giggling stream and scoop up a handful of pebbles. *Maybe I can throw my worries away with the stones.*

I toss one in.
Plunk.

Then another.
Plunk.

Then more.
Plunk, plink, plunk.

I reach into my pocket, rub my calming stone,
and remember splashing through streams
with Grandpa.

My worry-thoughts start feeling a little smoother.
But not all the way.

We keep hiking. Flowers tickle my shins.

Another worry itches my insides.

What if I miss Grandpa too much?

My heart pounds faster than rain on the roof.
My breath goes faster too.

Swisshhh...swishhh...

The breeze blows against my cheek.
Grandpa said that the sky breathes steady
and deep, and when we do too, our worries
can float away.

I look up at the blueness and the clouds.
I close my eyes. I take a deep breath,
inhaling through my nose, filling up my belly.
Then I exhale through my nose, slow and steady.

In...and out...

I feel better.
But all the worries
haven't drifted off yet.

Mom and Dad hike up ahead. I don't hurry.
I pass a big boulder with sparkly nuggets.
Grandpa taught me that nature is full of gifts.
And if we go slow, look, and listen, we can find them.

I crawl over a log. A spider scurries under it.

Grandpa said we can be like a spider's web...
flexible and strong all at once.

We come to a waterfall that pours straight down
from way up high.

Grandpa taught me that in nature, things change
and keep on flowing.

And things in our lives will change too.

All of the changes with moving feel like I'm standing under a waterfall of worries that's weighing down my shoulders.

What if my new guitar teacher isn't nice?

What if I get lost in my new school?

What if I never get used to our new house?

I rub my calming stone and take a big belly breath. My shoulders relax a little.

When we finally reach the top, the air is cooler
and crisper. We stand with the white-bark trees
whose tops have turned sun-bright yellow.

Mom and Dad walk to the edge to look out.
I sink to the ground where a big tree has fallen.
Tiny seedlings push through soft soil.

A new worry pushes into my thoughts. This worry is louder than all the others before. Louder even than thunder rumbling through the sky on a sticky summer night.

My heart feels like it moves into my throat.

What if...

I don't make new friends?

I feel like yelling and stomping and running.

But I don't.

Because I know what to do. Grandpa taught me.

I close my eyes,

    rub the calming stone in my fingers,

      and belly breathe.

I remember Grandpa's words before we left. "Sometimes I let my worries go by whispering them to the mountains."

So I start whispering.

I whisper and whisper and whisper into the breeze.

Tears squeeze out.

And after they've all leaked, and all the worries have been let go, I feel tired, like I've hiked up to the top of the tallest, steepest mountain of all.

A stream of sun lands just right on a spider's web.
The strands sparkle.

I feel stronger.

So I say to the web and the trees,

    and the mountain and the breeze...

        to everything...

"Thanks."

And then, just like Grandpa said, nature gives me a gift...
the wind blows the leaves into a dance, and the trees let
go a bucketful of color. They float down all around me
and blanket my lap. I giggle like the mountain stream.

I get up to join Mom and Dad.

I hear the stream and smell the pine cones.

I see so far that I think I can even see
the mountain that we shared with Grandpa.

And Grandpa was right.
Like the leaves that are falling,
things will continue to change...

But when the worry-thoughts come back,
I know what to do.

I'll rub my calming stone and think of
something that makes me feel thankful.

I'll breathe into my belly and out to the sky.

And I'll whisper my worries to the breeze.

Just like Grandpa taught me.

Author's Note

The boy in the story has a lot of worries on his mind about all of the changes in his life. His hike up the mountain with his parents reminds him of things his grandpa taught him. He is able to become more present in the moment by doing mindfulness exercises, which make him feel calmer and more peaceful. This is what mindfulness is about.

Mindfulness is great to practice even when you aren't worried or stressed. It helps you to notice and enjoy each moment more fully. Although being in nature is a wonderful place to be mindful and can help you feel peaceful, mindfulness can be practiced anywhere. If you begin to worry or feel anxious or your mind keeps racing, try these tips:

Belly Breathe
Fill your belly up like a balloon when you breathe in through your nose (inhale), and allow your belly to empty of the breath as you breathe out through your nose (exhale).

Think about Your Breath
Close your eyes and begin to think about your breath. Imagine the air coming in through your nose, then down through your lungs and filling up your belly, and then imagine it coming back out through your nose. Keep thinking about your breath like this. Your thoughts might like to wander, but gently tell your thoughts to come back to the breath.

Rub a Calming Stone
Holding something soothing in your hand, like a smooth stone, can make you feel calmer. Thinking about the feeling of the stone as you rub it can take your mind away from your worries.

Notice What Is Around You
Begin noticing what is happing in the present moment. Listen to the sounds, take in the smells, and feel what your body is feeling. This is a good way to help you stay in the present moment.

Feel Grateful
Allow yourself to feel grateful. Think of anything or anyone that makes you feel thankful. Allow all of those good, happy feelings to fill you up.

For all of the grandparents
in my life...I'm grateful for your
wisdom and guidance.—SM

This book is dedicated to
the sweetest grandpa ever:
Nonno Gino.—IU

Library of Congress Cataloging-in-Publication data is on file with the publisher.

Text copyright © 2021 by Sheri Mabry

Illustrations copyright © 2021 by Albert Whitman & Company

Illustrations by Ilaria Urbinati

First published in the United States of America in 2021 by Albert Whitman & Company

ISBN 978-0-8075-0614-1 (hardcover)

ISBN 978-0-8075-0620-2 (ebook)

Printed in China

10 9 8 7 6 5 4 3 2 1 WKT 26 25 24 23 22 21

Design by Aphelandra

For more information about Albert Whitman & Company,
visit our website at www.albertwhitman.com.